OPEN WORLD SQUAD

COUNTDOWN
▶▶ CRISIS ◀◀

BY MICHAEL ANTHONY STEELE

ILLUSTRATED BY MIKE LAUGHEAD

raintree
a Capstone company — publishers for children

Raintree is an imprint of Capstone Global Library Limited, a company incorporated in
England and Wales having its registered office at 264 Banbury Road, Oxford, OX2 7DY –
Registered company number: 6695582

Designed by Heidi Thompson
Original illustrations © Capstone Global Library Limited 2025
Originated by Capstone Global Library Ltd

978 1 3982 5747 4

British Library Cataloguing in Publication Data
A full catalogue record for this book is available from the British Library.

Printed and bound in India.

CONTENTS

CHAPTER 1
UNDERWATER ATTACK **8**

CHAPTER 2
EXPLOSIVE SURPRISE **15**

CHAPTER 3
PRESENTATION PANIC **19**

CHAPTER 4
PROBLEM SOLVING **24**

CHAPTER 5
TEAM TAKEDOWN **31**

CHAPTER 6
PRACTISE, PRACTISE, PRACTISE **37**

CHAPTER 7
CURRENT AFFAIRS **41**

CHAPTER 8
AIR SUPPLY **48**

CHAPTER 9
KAI'S TRAVEL AGENCY **56**

CHAPTER 10
STAR OF THE SHOW **60**

OPEN WORLD

In this online video game, players are free.
Be whatever avatar you want. Team up with
whoever you want. Choose any type of
mission you want! Fantasy adventure, battle
racing, sci-fi, action and more. So log on . . .

Open World awaits!

THE SQUAD

Kai

Screen name: K-EYE
Avatar: Techno-Ninja
Strengths: Supply, Stealth

Kai doesn't like being the centre of attention. He chose a role in OW where he can help others – in the background. His ninja avatar has many pockets to hold the squad's gear. Kai takes the job very seriously. He is quick to rush into a fight and pass out anything the group needs.

Hanna

Screen name: hanna_banana
Avatar: Elvin Archer
Strengths: Speed, Long-Range Attacks

Hanna is often busy with her school's drama department. She first joined OW to spend more time with her best friend, Zoe. In OW, she's great with a bow and arrow. Hanna is thrilled to take on a big role during the squad's attacks.

Mason

Screen name: MACE1
Avatar: Robo-Warrior
Strengths: Leadership,
Close-Range
Attacks

Mason knows the value of teamwork.
So he and his best friend, Kai, teamed up
in OW with cross-country friends Hanna
and Zoe. Mason has a strong avatar. But his
true strength? Acting as squad leader and
bringing together the players' many skills.

Zoe

Screen name: ZKatt
Avatar: Feline Wizard
Strengths: Spells,
Defence

Zoe is a tech wizard and OW expert.
She has been playing for the longest out
of everyone in the squad. Her avatar's
magic and defence skills help to keep the
group safe. Zoe isn't quite a pro gamer.
But she's close! Hundreds of followers
watch her live streams.

CHAPTER 1

UNDERWATER ATTACK

Kai hit a key on his keyboard. *TAK!*

On the computer screen, Kai's avatar ducked. A shark darted past. Kai breathed out. Its sharp teeth had barely missed him.

Of course, these weren't *ordinary* sharks. Teeth spun around the enemies' long noses like chain saws. One hit was enough to drop an avatar's health by half.

Nothing was ever ordinary in Open World. The online video game had an amazing mix of missions.

Kai and his squad had just begun this tricky underwater level. Each of their four avatars wore bulky diving suits. They walked heavily across the deep ocean floor. Their goal? Get to the city of Atlantis. Save it from an unknown threat.

MACE1: K! air plz

K-EYE: Coming!

Kai was on the move. Even before the chat box had popped up on his screen. Each avatar had a red health bar. In this mission, they also had a blue bar. It showed their air supply.

Kai's techno-ninja avatar was in charge of the squad's supplies. He gave out health. Ammo. And in this mission? Air. Kai had been scanning his team's air bars as they fought the sharks. Mason's was really short.

Kai threw a tank to his best friend. **FOOF!**

Mason's air bar shot up to full! His warrior avatar fired a speargun. **FFT!** A shark burst into bubbles.

MACE1: thx thse things r fast

hanna_banana: nk and we r soooooooooo slow!!!

Hanna's Elvin avatar could usually zip around with lightning speed. But not now. She was moving slowly. Really slowly. Underwater, they all were.

Hanna fired her own speargun. **FFT!** Direct hit!

hanna_banana: YESSSSS

ZKatt: incoming!

Zoe was the fourth squad member. Her cat-like avatar raised up a large seashell. **TUNK!** It blocked a fish.

Zoe's avatar was a wizard. But her spells were limited in this mission. She could only power up items. Like how she had strengthened the shell to be a shield.

Kai and Mason were friends in real life. But they only knew Hanna and Zoe from Open World. The four players had formed a squad to take on OW's many missions. They made a fantastic team.

hanna_banana: r we saving atlantis from sharks???

ZKatt: nah i bet theres a bigger boss to come. this is just wildlife

K-EYE: Crazy levelled up OW wildlife!

MACE1: lets finish them so we cn keep on to atlantis

Kai's heart raced as he tapped his keyboard. He moved his avatar towards Hanna's. She was low on air. If he didn't get her more? It'd be game over for Hanna.

FOOF! Kai threw Hanna a tank. Her blue bar refilled. In the next second, Hanna fired her speargun. The shot finished off the last enemy.

hanna_banana: thx!!!

MACE1: gg

Mason led them to a clear dome not far away. The domes were spaced along the ocean floor on the way to Atlantis. They were called "comfort zones". They were save points. And safe areas. Here, players could fill up on air. Pick up health. Ammo. Sometimes even find special weapons.

Everyone stepped into the comfort zone. Their helmets disappeared. Their air bars went to full. Kai got busy snatching up air tanks.

Mason raced over to a large net gun.

MACE1: SWEET! new weapon! any1 mind if i grab it?

hanna_banana: im sticking with the speargun. not as good as my bow but close!!!

ZKatt: still shielding 4 me. K?

K-EYE: Nope I'm good.

hanna_banana: ya K is alrdy the big hero this mission with air supply!

"No kidding," Kai muttered.

Kai didn't like being the centre of attention. In real life or OW. That was why he always took on the supply role. But now? Underwater? Everyone needed extra air tanks. He played a more vital role than ever before.

Kai jumped as his screen suddenly went red. Bright numbers appeared above the zone's exit. They counted down from ten.

ZKatt: guess we r not supposed 2 stay in here 4 long

K-EYE: Yup. Time to step out of our comfort zone.

hanna_banana: ha!!!

ZKatt: lol

MACE1: good 1 dude

Kai sighed as he followed the others. With his more important role, he really *was* stepping out of his comfort zone.

CHAPTER 2

EXPLOSIVE SURPRISE

The squad trudged across the ocean floor. Nothing rushed up to attack. The waters were clear.

MACE1: stay frosty

hanna_banana: u know it

ZKatt: awwww so cute!

A small, big-eyed fish swam up to Zoe. Its tiny fins flapped quickly as it circled her. A second big-eyed fish came over. Then a third. Then a fourth. Soon, a school of tiny fish swam around the squad.

MACE1: r we suppsed to fight them?

hanna_banana: they r 2 cute 2 fight :)

Hanna's avatar moved closer to one of the fish.

ZKatt: nonono

K-EYE: IT'S A TRAP!

WHOMP!

As soon as Hanna had touched the tiny fish, it ballooned to five times its size. Sharp spikes covered its round body. It was a puffer fish!

But nothing was ever ordinary in Open World. This puffer fish's spikes shot off.

PFT! PFT-PFT-PFT-PFT! PFT!

Everyone was hit by the tiny missiles. Kai cringed as their health bars dropped.

Worse, the spikes hit two other puffer fish. **_WHOMP! WHOMP!_** Those fish ballooned. They shot spikes. They hit other fish. **_WHOMP!_**

It was a chain reaction! Sharp spikes shot in from all sides.

> **hanna_banana:** AAAAAAAAAAAA
>
> **ZKatt:** 2 me! shield!

Everyone crowded behind Zoe's shield. The large shell blocked the spikes. But only from one direction. The squad's health dropped even lower.

Kai got busy. He passed out med packs.

Mason fired his net launcher. Hanna worked her speargun. More puffers kept coming.

> **K-EYE:** Almost out of med packs!
>
> **hanna_banana:** out of spears! not so cute any more!!

ZKatt: we r toast if we stay here

MACE1: run 4 it!

The squad ran from the school of killer puffer fish. But the spikes moved so fast. And the avatars moved so slowly. Everyone's health dropped as they took more hits.

Kai closed in on Hanna. Her health was almost empty. He was about to throw a med pack. Then a bright red window popped up on his screen.

DING!

▶▶▶ 3 days before presentation ◀◀◀

Kai's hands fell away from the keyboard. His chest tightened, and his mouth went dry. Beads of sweat formed on his forehead. He had trouble catching his breath. It was the start of a full-blown panic attack.

CHAPTER 3

PRESENTATION PANIC

Kai closed his eyes. He focused on his breathing. He breathed in through his nose. Out through his mouth. In and out. Long and slow.

He could already feel his heart beating slower. His breathing came more easily.

Kai was no stranger to panic attacks. He had been having them for years. A school counsellor had taught him how to deal with them. In theory, his system could stop the attacks before they started. It worked *most* of the time.

Kai opened his eyes. The Open World logo filled his screen. He groaned.

The game had ended. The puffer fish must have finished him off when he had stopped moving. Did the others make it to the next comfort zone? Kai hoped so.

Bzz! Kai looked at his phone. It was a text from Mason.

u ok?

yeah, meet in OWM

Kai logged back into the game. Soon his avatar was standing in OWM. The Open World Market.

The huge market spread out behind Kai. Other players were busy shopping. Here, people could buy gear for all OW's levels. Laser blasters for sci-fi. Vehicle upgrades for racing. Spells for fantasy. There were even character skins for sale.

Mason's avatar walked over. He no longer wore the diving suit. He had his basic character skin. A warrior with a funky robot head.

Kai's ninja was dressed normally too. A mask covered his face. A hood was pulled over his head. Only the avatar's eyes showed. As embarrassed as Kai felt, his character was dressed perfectly.

MACE1: what happened?

K-EYE: Panic attack

MACE1: oh

K-EYE: It's over now.

As Kai's best friend, Mason knew all about the panic attacks. He had been with Kai a couple of times when they had happened.

MACE1: the game 2 tense? we cud do another level

K-EYE: No. It's the project.

MACE1: thot u finished

K-EYE: The research isn't the problem.

MACE1: oh yeah

Mason also knew about Kai's shyness. Kai hated speaking in front of groups. And that was what this project was all about. Presenting.

Their teacher, Mrs Meehan, had given the class a geography project. They had to choose a European country and give a presentation. *Choose* wasn't the right word. They had drawn countries from a hat.

MACE1: dnt worry yull do great dude

K-EYE: Easy for you. You got Italy. Not boring Malta.

MACE1: so ur talk will b shorter. not much 2 say = less time in front of evryone!

An image of Kai standing in front of the class flashed through his head. He shivered. His heart began to race. Kai decided to change the subject.

K-EYE: Were H and Z mad I tilted?

MACE1: nope jst wondering wht happend. we did all die tho

K-EYE: Sorry

MACE1: not ur fault, we were pwned by cute fish lol

K-EYE: Try again tomorrow?

MACE1: u bet! l8er!

Kai logged out of OW. He leaned back in his chair. He breathed. In and out. Long and slow.

"Kai, dinner!" his brother, Noa, shouted from the hallway. "Play with your made-up computer friends later."

Kai rolled his eyes. "Coming."

But he sat there for a moment longer. He kept at his slow breathing. He tried to think of anything but the project. It wasn't working.

CHAPTER 4

PROBLEM SOLVING

The next evening, Kai met the squad in OW.
They restarted the underwater level. They were back
in a comfort zone. The one before the killer puffer fish.

K-EYE: Sorry I tilted yesterday.

ZKatt: everything ok?

K-EYE: Big school project

hanna_banana: u need 2 go???

K-EYE: No, project is done. Just stressing over the presentation. Two days away now.

MACE1: has 2 tlk about malta

ZKatt: the country?

K-EYE: Yup. It's super boring. Plus talking in front of the class is the worst.

hanna_banana: totes get it. i still get butterflies b4 shows!

K-EYE: Really?

MACE1: thot u been in drama 4 evr, ur the big star

hanna_banana: somtimes. i do things that help tho

Just then, the lights in the zone went red.

The countdown began. 10, 9, 8, 7 . . .

Kai let out a sigh of relief. He was happy to change the subject. After all, if even *Hanna* still got nervous? What chance did he have?

MACE1: rdy squad?

ZKatt: ttly!

hanna_banana: >:)

K-EYE: Ready!

MACE1: and no touching the fish H

hanna_banana: lol right

They left the comfort zone. Like before, a little puffer fish swam over. Then another. And another.

hanna_banana: soooo cute tho!!!

ZKatt: H!

hanna_banana: jk :D

The squad slowly made their way forwards. They dodged the tiny fish.

Kai watched everyone's air and health more closely than ever. He couldn't let his squad down again.

A dome came into view. The next comfort zone!

But the puffers weren't going to make things easy. Two fish bumped into each other. **WHOMP!** **WHOMP!** They ballooned up.

MACE1: RUN

Everyone moved as fast as the underwater setting let them. The chain reaction had already begun. Spikes flew everywhere!

Zoe moved to the back. She held up her shield. She blocked most of the spikes.

But the running was really using up their air. Kai's heart raced as he passed out tanks. The squad finally dashed into the dome.

Luckily, there were plenty of air tanks in the new comfort zone. Kai grabbed as many as he could carry.

MACE1: that was close

K-EYE: Yeah, hard to keep up with air supply.

ZKatt: ur doin awesome! pro gamer moves!

K-EYE: Thnx

MACE1: hey Z any tips 4 K? talkin n front of ppl?

hanna_banana: ya! girl talks to 100s every day!

K-EYE: Seriously dude?

Kai knew that Mason was only trying to help. But one of the reasons Kai liked OW? He could forget about the real world. Stuff like the project. In OW, he could be whoever he wanted. Not someone who was scared to talk in front of people.

Then again, maybe Zoe could help. She *did* live stream to lots of followers all the time.

K-EYE: OK fine. I'll take all the help I can get.

ZKatt: its kinda different tho. im not rly in front of people

hanna_banana: but still! 100s!!!

K-EYE: You don't get scared?

ZKatt: was at first but then i pretended i was only talking to H. hlped a lot!

MACE1: u cud pretend its just me n class K

K-EYE: I guess

hanna_banana: M in same class? whats ur country?

MACE1: italy

hanna_banana: ooolala! bonjure!!!

ZKatt: lol thats france

hanna_banana: lol! pizza!!! lasagna!!!

MACE1: lol

K-EYE: LOL!

Kai really did laugh out loud. It was the first time he had thought about his presentation without freaking out. He wondered if Zoe's advice would really work. Could it be that simple?

Just then, the countdown began. 10, 9, 8 . . .

hanna_banana: WOOO! lets do this!!!

ZKatt: lol save that energy 4 when we get 2 atlantis

hanna_banana: i have enuf 4 the whole game!!!

The squad left the zone. They didn't have to wait for their next challenge. A giant sea snake swam in to attack!

CHAPTER 5

TEAM TAKEDOWN

The sea snake roared. It bared a mouthful of teeth as it swam forwards. Then it sliced at the squad with the sharp fins on its head.

TUNK! Zoe blocked the attack with her shield. It kept her and Hanna safe. But Mason and Kai took a hit. Their health dropped.

Hanna fired her speargun. **FFT! FFT!** The beast swam back into the darkness.

hanna_banana: ???

K-EYE: We should keep moving. Gonna run out of air.

They took a few slow steps. The snake returned. It rushed in to attack.

Hanna fired. Hit! Hit! Miss!

The beast struck back. Hanna couldn't move away in time. Its fins slammed into her. Her health dropped by half.

Then the snake swam away.

The squad trudged on. Kai worked on passing out med packs and air.

hanna_banana: its so fast!!!

ZKatt: mybe yur net can slow it down M?

MACE1: i can try

When the serpent came back again, Mason aimed his net gun. **FOOP!**

The net wrapped around the beast's head. The sea snake twisted back and forth.

MACE1: YES! go go go

Zoe and Hanna stepped up. Zoe raised her shield to block the beast's thrashing. Hanna fired her speargun.

FFT-FFT! FFT-FFT!

All four shots hit their target. But the snake didn't go down. It continued to struggle against the net. It was breaking free!

Kai ran to Hanna with more spears. She kept firing. Kai had just handed her the last spear when –

BOOOM!

The beast went down. It sunk away into the ocean floor.

ZKatt: wO0t!!

K-EYE: Yay!

MACE1: YES! gg H

hanna_banana: thx u2!!!

Kai checked the squad's air levels. They all needed some. He passed out the last of it.

K-EYE: Sorry to be a downer. But we need to move. Out of air tanks.

MACE1: lets go then. just a few more stops till atlantis!

The squad walked to the next comfort zone. Their air lasted just long enough to get inside.

ZKatt: can we call it? got a live stream comin up

MACE1: yeah and i got homewrk

ZKatt: good hustle K. And ur gonna do fine on ur project.

K-EYE: We'll see. But thnx for the advice.

hanna_banana: hey i gnt another good tip 2 try

K-EYE: ?

hanna_banana: practise practise practise!!!

K-EYE: ??

hanna_banana: b4 a play i know my lines front to back. so much less stress when im super prepared!

K-EYE: True. That's why I always finish my homework asap.

MACE1: i alwys wait 2 last minute

ZKatt: lol gonna loose game time if ur not careful

hanna_banana: yeah then we'll have 2 find a new squad leader!

K-EYE: Maybe Devon can cover for you.

MACE1: lol yeah right my little bro has got nothin on me

ZKatt: k cu!

hanna_banana: BYE!!!

MACE1: l8tr

One by one, the avatars faded away. Kai was about to log off too. But he stopped. He looked around the zone. Something was different.

Then it hit him. This zone didn't have as many supplies as the last one. Fewer air tanks. Fewer spears and nets.

It looked as if OW was ramping up the stress level. Whether Kai wanted it or not.

CHAPTER 6

PRACTISE, PRACTISE, PRACTISE

Kai stepped away from his computer. He might as well take Hanna's advice. It was time to practise.

Kai pulled a stack of note cards from his school bag. He stood in front of his dresser mirror and cleared his throat. He read the first card.

"The country of Malta is made up of five islands. It's in the Mediterranean Sea," he said. "Its capital is Valletta. Its population is over five hundred thousand."

Kai looked up. In the mirror, he could see sweat on his forehead. His cheeks turned red.

"The official languages are . . ." Kai shook his head. He turned away from the mirror. Watching himself was too embarrassing.

"The official languages are Maltese and English," he continued.

Kai's eyes fell on his computer screen. It showed the OW logo. He thought about Zoe's advice. Pretend to talk just to Mason. Kai sighed. Saying all this stuff to his friend would be embarrassing too. But maybe not as bad as to the whole class.

Kai picked up his phone. He texted Mason.

Vid chat?

k

Soon, Kai got a video chat invite. He accepted it, and Mason's face filled his phone screen.

"What's up, dude?" Mason asked.

Kai rubbed his neck. "Can you, um, watch my presentation?" he asked. "If I'm going to pretend to be talking just to you, then I'd better practise."

"Sure," Mason said with a shrug. "But I wasn't kidding about homework."

"It won't take long," Kai said. "Like you said. It's Malta. There's not much to say."

"Then go for it," Mason said.

Kai placed the phone on his desk. He pulled out his note cards and began again.

Kai kept looking up at Mason as he read off his facts. Zoe was right. Talking to his friend was easier. Even easier than talking to himself in the mirror. If he could keep his eyes on Mason during class, he just might get through this.

"Malta has hot, dry summers," Kai read. "And short, cool winters."

Kai looked up again. Mason was pointing.

"What?" Kai asked.

But Mason wasn't pointing at Kai. He was pointing to something behind him. Kai spun around.

Noa was standing in the bedroom doorway. The sixteen-year-old covered his mouth, trying not to smile.

Kai's eyes widened. "Noa?!"

His older brother burst out laughing. "Man, can you come to my room tonight and do that?" Noa asked. "I've been having trouble sleeping, and that talk will knock me right out!"

Kai's face got hot with embarrassment. Any confidence he had gained washed away in a flash.

CHAPTER 7

CURRENT AFFAIRS

The next night, the squad met at their last save point. The comfort zone with fewer supplies. Kai picked up ten air tanks. That was all.

DING!

►►► 1 day before presentation ◄◄◄

Kai closed the reminder. He blew out a breath and tried not to think about it. But Hanna must've been reading his mind somehow.

hanna_banana: hows the project K?

K-EYE: Don't want to talk about it plz.

hanna_banana: ?

MACE1: K's bro saw him practising

ZKatt: ouch

K-EYE: He's a pain sometimes. Let's just get going.

MACE1: sure evryone rdy?

hanna_banana: u know it!!

Kai was glad to get back to the game. He led the way out of the comfort zone.

Tiny fish darted around the squad. The fish didn't attack. Nothing did. No sea creatures, at least.

FWOOOSH!

An invisible force pushed everyone to the right.

hanna_banana: WHT WUZ THAT

MACE1: strng current?

FWOOOSH!

Another current came in. But from the left. Everyone staggered. Kai had to fight to keep his avatar moving forward.

> **ZKatt:** crazy!

> **hanna_banana:** its better than spiky puffers or jerky big brothers!!!

> **K-EYE:** LOL. But we're slower than ever now. Using more air.

> **MACE1:** just gotta power thru

The currents kept coming. They hit from all sides.

Kai kept an eye on the squad's air. He passed out a tank when someone was low. He was so focused that he almost didn't notice a clue.

> **K-EYE:** Hey watch the fish!

> **hanna_banana:** ???

> **K-EYE:** They swim in the direction of the next current.

Sure enough, the tiny fish began swimming left. Then a wave struck. From the left. The fish swam *against* the current!

> **ZKatt:** nice catch K!

> **MACE1:** good 2 know cuz look!

Up ahead, the path thinned. Two giant valleys opened on either side of it. A current could push an avatar right over the edge. Since the squad wore bulky diving suits, they would sink into darkness.

But since Kai had pointed out the fish, they were ready. They stepped onto the thin path. When the fish turned, the players knew how to fight the current.

FWOOSH! FWOOSH! FWOOSH! FWOOSH!

They fought through four waves. Finally, they passed the valleys. The path widened again. Kai let out the breath he was holding.

The next comfort zone came into view. The squad filed inside.

ZKatt: gg K!

hanna_banana: TTLY! also K dont listen 2 ur bro!! what did the pain say anywy?

Kai sighed. Hanna wasn't letting it go.

K-EYE: Said it was boring. Could put him to sleep.

ZKatt: >:(

K-EYE: He's not wrong. It's Malta. My presentation is gonna be a disaster.

MACE1: can u mke it less boring somehow?

K-EYE: Yeah right

hanna_banana: WAIT!! i hve an idea!!! pretend ur a travl agent!! b rly excited about malta!

Kai felt his face get hot. He typed quickly.

K-EYE: NO WAY! I'll look like a loser! Everyone will laugh at me!

hanna_banana: thats the point!!! will b funny if ur rly trying 2 sell it

ZKatt: yeah!! the more boring the better!

MACE1: not a bad idea dude

K-EYE: I don't know

The lights in the zone went red. Kai looked for the countdown. But it didn't come. Instead, the room began filling with water.

Kai's breath caught in his throat. This new twist, along with Hanna's suggestion, was making him more nervous than ever.

CHAPTER 8

AIR SUPPLY

Water poured into the room. Kai pushed the presentation out of his mind. He had to focus on the game. It was stressful enough. He scrambled to gather supplies. It didn't take long. There were even fewer air tanks than the last zone. Still, the room was nearly full of water as Kai and the others rushed outside.

hanna_banana: no more warning? no countdown???

MACE1: guess not

ZKatt: um guys look

The sea floor was covered with crumbled buildings. Broken spears and shields lay all around.

K-EYE: Is this Atlantis?

ZKatt: cant b, we r supposed 2 save it

MACE1: must b edge of the city. we r close!

hanna_banana: then lets GOOOO

The group stepped through the ruins. Kai picked up some of the broken weapons. But they were useless.

Then he spotted something useful. A full air tank! Kai grabbed it.

Suddenly, an enemy rushed out of a wrecked building. It was two sea creatures in one. The front? The deadly jaws of a shark. The back? Eight long arms of an octopus.

Zoe quickly raised her shield. **TUNK!** She blocked the attack.

Hanna fired her speargun. Hit! The beast didn't go down. Instead, it shot out black ink. It swam off as the ink spread around the squad.

MACE1: octoshark?!

hanna_banana: yeah and now i cant c!!!

ZKatt: same

Two octosharks suddenly burst through the black cloud. No one had time to react.

CHOMP! The avatars' health dropped by half.

Kai passed out med packs. Mason raised his net gun. **FOOP!**

The net trapped an octoshark. But it just blasted more ink. So did the other one before swimming away.

The ink cloud widened. Kai's screen was almost totally black.

MACE1: gotta move! get thru the ink!!

Kai kept his avatar going forwards. The scene slowly brightened.

The squad picked up speed. Kai was worried about all the air they were using. Luckily, he found two tanks in the rubble.

More octosharks attacked. Hanna and Mason fought them off. The squad ran before ink filled the area. The next comfort zone came into view.

Then Kai saw something else. Mason's air supply was almost empty!

Kai gritted his teeth. How had he missed it? He raced over to his friend.

Two more octosharks darted in. Zoe blocked one with her shield. The other zeroed in on Kai.

Hanna fired a spear at it. Miss!

Kai kept moving. He could take a hit. But he had to get his friend air.

The octoshark dashed forwards to bite. In the same instant, Kai threw the tank.

WHOMP! The octoshark swallowed the tank whole!

Hanna aimed at the beast.

FWIIIT! VOOOOOOM!

Hanna's spear, plus the air tank in its belly, made the enemy explode.

There was no time to celebrate. The squad's air bars were almost empty. They darted into the comfort zone.

Kai's heart was pounding as he looked around. The new zone was beaten up. It was as if whatever threat was attacking Atlantis had hit here too. The squad had to be close to the end of the level.

MACE1: WOW how cool wuz that??

hanna_banana: SO COOL. shoulda been feeding tanks to fishys the whole time!!!

ZKatt: THATS why the xtra tanks were lying round!

K-EYE: I thought they were for all the running.

MACE1: rdy 2 finish this?

Kai stared at the screen. His heart was racing again. But not because of OW.

K-EYE: Can't. Have to get ready for tomorrow.

MACE1: right. tmrw night then. u got it dude!

ZKatt: good luck K, u will rock the presentation!

K-EYE: Thnx

Just before Kai signed off, he received a DM. It was Hanna.

hanna_banana: hey! i have some ideas about the travel agent thing

K-EYE: I really don't think I can do that.

hanna_banana: u can!!! u will b gr8!!!

K-EYE: It's just

K-EYE: I get panic attacks. I get them just THINKING about talking in front of people

hanna_banana: perfect!!!

K-EYE: what?!!

hanna_banana: ooooof. sorry. didn't mean 2 b a jerk. that sucks. srsly

K-EYE: Tell me about it.

hanna_banana: i just meant this character is supposed 2 b nervous. so taking time 2 breathe works for character and u

K-EYE: That is what I do to stop my panic attacks.

hanna_banana: see? its meant 2 b! wut do u think??

K-EYE: I don't know.

hanna_banana: it will SO work!!! i promise! and i'll help, i got yur back

K-EYE: All right

Kai got a video chat invite. He accepted, and Hanna's grinning face appeared.

CHAPTER 9

KAI'S TRAVEL AGENCY

The next day, Kai fidgeted at his school desk.
He pulled at his collar. Hanna had suggested he wear
a suit and tie. As a costume. Now Kai felt like he
was soaked with sweat. He tapped nervously on the
briefcase he had borrowed from his dad. A prop for his
talk. Another suggestion from Hanna.

The night before, Hanna had listened to Kai's talk.
Then she had showed him how to tweak it into a travel
agent pitch. It had actually been pretty easy. She had
told him where to pause. What to focus on.

Kai had made changes. He had run it again. Got more tips. Made more changes.

Hanna had been thrilled with the results. Kai just hoped he lived up to her expectations.

Kai had sat through four other presentations so far. He couldn't remember what they were about. He had been too busy going over his note cards.

A thought suddenly popped into his head. What if they didn't get to his presentation today? He would have to wait another whole day. Maybe two!

Kai felt his heart race. He had trouble breathing. A panic attack was on the way.

Kai closed his eyes. He breathed. In and out. Long and slow.

It was working. Breathing got easier. He was not going to have a panic attack. Not when he was so close.

"Kai?" a voice asked. "Earth to Kai."

His eyes popped open. He had not noticed Mrs Meehan talking to him.

"Are you ready to present?" the teacher asked. "You certainly seem dressed for the part."

The other students laughed. Kai felt the panic rise up again. He glanced over at Mason.

His best friend mouthed, *"You've got this."*

Kai breathed. In and out. But he felt numb as he shuffled to the front of the class. He placed his briefcase on the teacher's desk. He looked at Mason.

"Hello," he said. His voice cracked. "I'm Kai. With Kai's Travel Agency." He opened his case. A sign on the lid read: Kai's Travel Agency.

The class laughed. As Hanna had instructed, Kai made a big show of pointing to the sign. More laughs.

Kai let out a shaky breath. He felt better. Not much, but a little.

"I'm a bit nervous," Kai said. "It's my first day on the job." That got another laugh.

He cleared his throat. "On your next holiday, go to the lovely island nation of . . . Malta!" He pulled out a map and waved a hand over it. Another laugh.

"Visit . . . our lovely capital, Valletta," he continued. "Where you can speak English or practise your Maltese." That also got a laugh.

"See . . . our amazing wildlife." He pulled out two photos. "The white-toothed shrew and . . . the lesser horseshoe bat. Very exciting." More laughter.

Kai's biggest fears had come true. He had stood in front of the class. Everyone had laughed at him. But when they were *supposed* to laugh, it wasn't so bad.

Mason grinned and gave a thumbs-up. Kai smiled back and continued his presentation.

CHAPTER 10

STAR OF THE SHOW

That night, the squad met in the final comfort zone. There were hardly any supplies to gather. But that wasn't the big news.

MACE1: u shuda seen him! K was the star of the show!!!

hanna_banana: <3 <3 <3 i knew it!!!

ZKatt: woohoo!!!

K-EYE: Not true

MACE1: YES TRU! wuz best n class 4sure

ZKatt: u shoulda recorded it!!

K-EYE: NOOOO!!! I would've died!

hanna_banana: so happy 4 u K

K-EYE: Thnx fnr your help. Really.

hanna_banana: np :)

MACE1: ppl going tmrw will have 2 up their game. ncluding me!

hanna_banana: u shud order pizza!!! 4 italy!

K-EYE: lol sounds good to me

The lights turned red. The room began filling with water.

MACE1: ready to go save atlantis?

K-EYE: YES!

ZKatt: SO ready!

hanna_banana: best squad EVR 2 the rescue!!!

The players filed out of the comfort zone. The shining towers of Atlantis rose high into the waters above them.

But black ink clouds hung between the buildings. Octosharks were attacking the city! Atlantean warriors chased the beasts. They rode past on giant sea horses. The squad had walked right into a war zone!

hanna_banana: should we help these guys???

MACE1: dont think so. the path leads ovr there

The squad followed Mason through the underwater city. Zoe blocked a few octoshark attacks with her shield. But the enemies were mostly focused on the Atlanteans.

Kai found more air tanks along the way. Med packs and spears too. Plenty were lying around.

That could only mean one thing. The big boss was coming.

Finally, Mason stopped.

MACE1: theres our target

ZKatt: oh boy

Kai gulped as a cut scene filled his computer screen. The video clip showed the mother of all octosharks. It was enormous. The beast smashed buildings with its eight arms. It snapped its teeth at Atlanteans riding by as if they were flies.

The scene ended. Kai's screen showed their four avatars standing in front of the huge enemy.

hanna_banana: plan???

K-EYE: Look around. There are air tanks everywhere!

ZKatt: feed it and then boom, like last time?

K-EYE: Has to be.

MACE1: ready K?

K-EYE: Me???

MACE1: u can carry the most. we will distract, u feed it!

hanna_banana: u can do it K!!!

Kai's heart raced. His knee bounced. This entire mission had relied on him more and more. Now? For the final battle? He was key. And just like his presentation, all eyes were on him.

Kai took a few deep breaths to focus. His friends moved into position.

FFWT! Hanna fired her speargun. It didn't do any damage. But it did get the enemy's attention.

The octoshark leaned closer. It swiped a giant arm.

The squad jumped. After the arm had passed, Kai ran closer.

FOOF-FOOF-FOOF-FOOF-FOOF!

He flung five air tanks at the big octoshark. They went right down its throat.

The beast didn't seem to care. It swung another long arm.

Kai jumped again. Then he ran around grabbing more tanks. He threw them into the beast's mouth. **FOOF! FOOF!** He lost track of how many tanks he had fed it. Soon, there were no more.

K-EYE: That's all!

MACE1: ur up H!

hanna_banana: AW YEAH

Hanna aimed her speargun. **FWIIIT!**

The spear zipped toward the monster's belly. It looked so tiny. It didn't seem as if it would do anything at all. Then –

KA-VOOOOOOOOM!!!

The creature exploded. Huge chunks of octoshark went flying everywhere. The Atlanteans cheered.

hanna_banana: YAY!!! atlantis is saaaaaved

K-EYE: We did it!

ZKatt: WOOHOO!

MACE1: YAAA MAN! gg evrybody! gg K!

K-EYE: Thnx!

hanna_banana: 2 wins for K today!!!

Kai let out a long breath. Hanna was right.

He had stepped out of his comfort zone twice today.

With success each time! Kai grinned.

MACE1: so how about a victry speech K?

ZKatt: lol thot u were his friend M?

hanna_banana: go K go!! yull be great as usual!!!

K-EYE: LOL thnx but I'm good. Just ready for the next OW mission!

BONUS ROUND

1. Describe why Kai was nervous about the underwater level. Use examples to support your answer. If he didn't also have the school presentation coming up, do you think he'd feel differently about the OW mission?

2. Hanna said she still gets butterflies before acting on stage. Why do you think this surprised Kai and Mason?

3. Kai's friends supported him as he got ready for his presentation. Which piece of advice do you think was most helpful? Why?

4. At first, Kai didn't want to talk about his problem with his friends. Think of a time when you needed help dealing with something stressful. Do you find it hard or easy to ask for help? How did you feel after asking?

5. Imagine if Kai's presentation hadn't gone so well. How do you think his friends would have reacted to the news? What would they say? Write out the chat.

6. When you feel really nervous, what are the things you do that help you to calm down? Make a list.

TAKING CARE

In real life, there may not be levels to beat. Or bosses to battle. But it can still be tough. Equip yourself with the tools and knowledge to take care of your mental health. Check out the online resources below. And don't ever be afraid to ask for help from friends, family or trusted adults.

BBC Bitesize:
www.bbc.co.uk/bitesize/articles/zmvt6g8

BBC Children in Need:
www.bbcchildreninneed.co.uk

Childline:
www.childline.org.uk

Health For Teens:
www.healthforteens.co.uk

Mental Health Foundation:
www.mentalhealth.org.uk

NHS Mental Health:
www.nhs.uk/mental-health/children-and-young-adults/mental-health-support/

Young Minds:
www.youngminds.org.uk/young-person/

GLOSSARY

advice ideas on what to do about a problem

avatar character in a video game, chat room, app or other computer program that stands for and is controlled by a person

chain reaction series of events where each event causes the next one

comfort zone activity or setting in which you feel comfortable and in control and that doesn't worry you

current steady and ongoing movement of some of the water in a river, lake or ocean

dome building that is shaped like half of a ball

embarrassed feeling silly, uncomfortable or foolish in front of others

explode blow apart with a loud bang and great force

focus keep all your attention on something

mission planned job or task

presentation talk giving information about something

trudge walk heavily and slowly

vital very important

THE AUTHOR

MICHAEL ANTHONY STEELE has been in the entertainment industry for more than 27 years, writing for television, films and video games. He has written more than 120 books for exciting characters and brands, including Batman, Superman, Wonder Woman, Spider-Man, Shrek and Scooby-Doo. Steele lives on a ranch in Texas, USA, but he enjoys meeting readers when he goes to visit schools and libraries across the United States. For more information, visit MichaelAnthonySteele.com.

THE ILLUSTRATOR

MIKE LAUGHEAD is a comics creator and illustrator of children's books, T-shirts, book covers and other fun things in the children's market. He has been doing that for almost 20 years. Mike is also an illustration instructor at Brigham Young University-Idaho, USA. He lives in Idaho with his amazing wife and three wonderful daughters. To see his portfolio, visit shannonassociates.com/mikelaughead

▶▶ READ THEM ALL! ◀◀